For Huckleberry

Special thanks to Bill Jones and the uniquely splendid Spring Grove School in Wye, Kent, England

Thanks to Debra Roldan

Text copyright © 2016 by Suzanne Lang
Jacket art and interior illustrations copyright © 2016 by Max Lang

All rights reserved. Published in the United States by Random House Children's Books,
a division of Penguin Random House LLC, New York.

Random House and the colophon are registered trademarks of Penguin Random House LLC.

Visit us on the Web! randomhousekids.com

Educators and librarians, for a variety of teaching tools, visit us at
RHTeachersLibrarians.com

Library of Congress Cataloging-in-Publication Data
Lang, Suzanne.
Hooray for kids! / by Suzanne Lang & Max Lang. — First edition.
pages cm
Summary: Illustrations and simple, rhyming text celebrate the uniqueness of each child.
ISBN 978-0-553-53783-3 (hardcover) — ISBN 978-0-553-53784-0 (hardcover library binding) — ISBN 978-0-553-53785-7 (ebook)
[1. Stories in rhyme. 2. Individuality—Fiction.] I. Lang, Max, illustrator. II. Title.
PZ8.3.L27672Kid 2016 [E]—dc23 2014047330

Book design by John Sazaklis

MANUFACTURED IN CHINA

10 9 8 7 6 5 4 3 2 1

First Edition

HOORAY FOR KIDS!

by
Suzanne Lang
&
Max Lang

Random House 🏠 New York

Some kids are good at math.

Some kids need lots of sleep.

Some kids run real fast.

Some kids love to eat.

Some kids play video games.
Some kids speak German.
Some kids paint a lot.

Some kids are named Herman.

Some kids dig the sand.
Some kids do the crawl.

Some kids pick their nose
and roll it in a ball.

Some kids keep lots of ants.
Some kids collect rocks.

Some kids always wear boots.
Some go with sandals and socks.

Some kids jump real high.

Others crawl real low.

Some kids brush their hair
and tie it in a bow.

Some kids are sloppy.
Some kids are neat.

Some kids chew their food so you can see what they eat.

But whether you're

a fall kid,

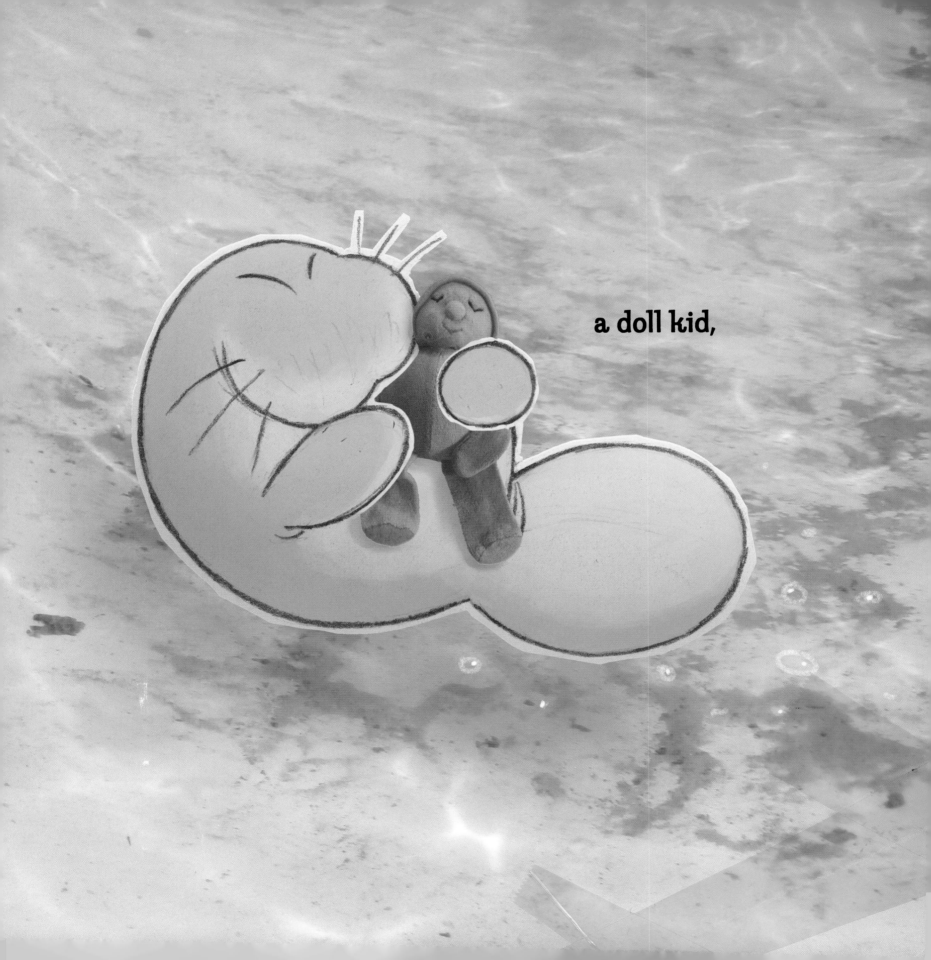

a doll kid,

a play-a-lot-of-ball kid,

a shy kid,

a pie kid,

an
always-asking-why
kid,

a clown kid,

a gown kid,

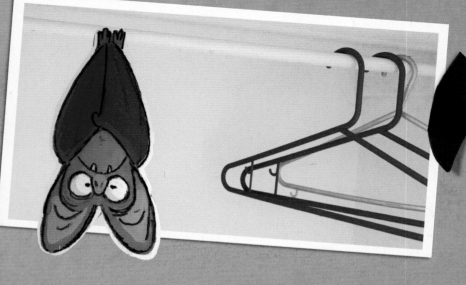

an
upside-down-frown
kid,

a surly kid,

a twirly kid,

a wake-up-nice-
and-early kid,

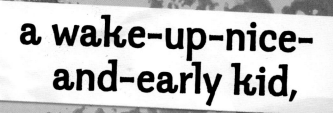

a skate kid,

a late kid,

a lift-a-lot-
of-weight kid,

a book kid,

a hook kid,

a really-loves-
to-cook kid,

to all kids we say,

each one of you is special.
KID, KID, HOORAY!

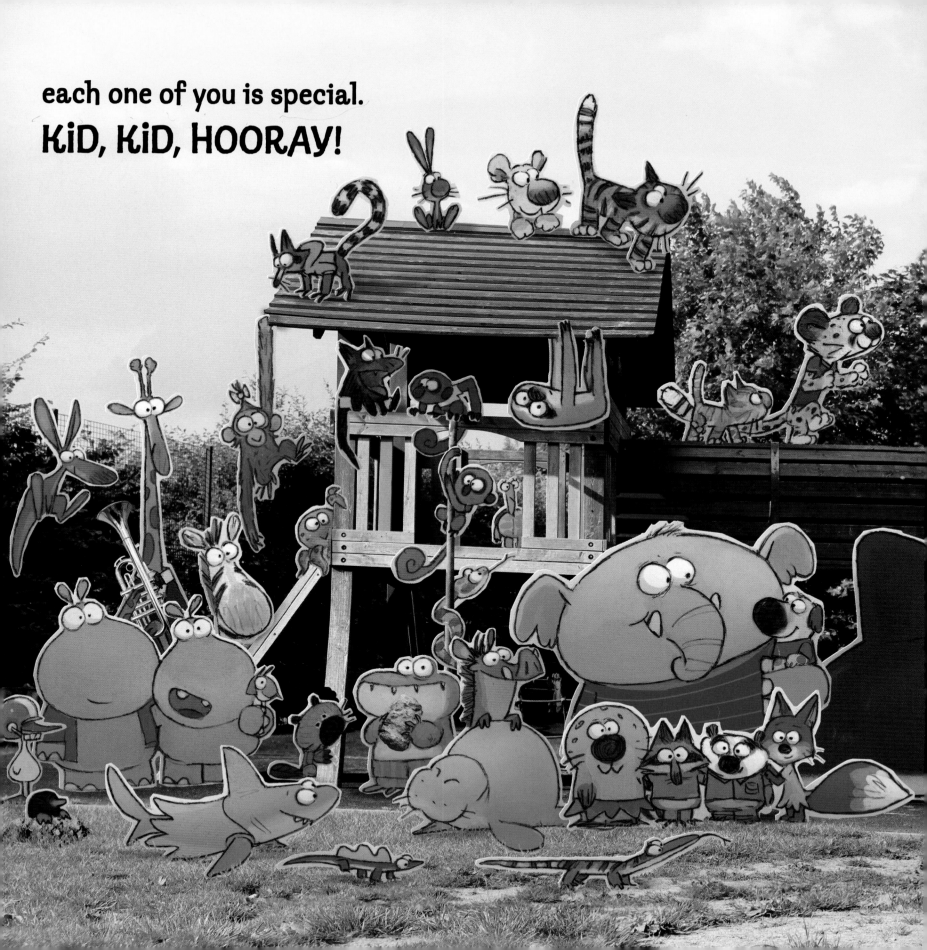